First published 1980 by
Octopus Books Limited
59 Grosvenor Street
London W1

© 1980 Octopus Books Limited

ISBN 0 7064 1362 8

Produced by Mandarin Publishers Limited
22a Westland Road, Quarry Bay, Hong Kong

Printed in Hong Kong

Educational and Series advisor Felicia Law

PDO 79-413

The
Ballet Class

by
Felicia Law and Judy Brason

illustrated by
Sally Launder

octopus

Emma and Jo were best friends. They were in the same class at Mayflower School. They walked to school together each day. They worked together, played together and were sometimes a nuisance together.

Emma had her hair in long pigtails. So did Jo. Today Jo is going to her first ballet lesson.

'Mummy?' says Emma.

'I know, I know,' says Mrs Daley, 'You two have to do everything together, don't you? However, first we had better have a long talk about ballet lessons and make sure you understand what ballet is all about.'

'It's the Big Game on television tonight, Dad,' says Emma's brother Tom.

'I was looking forward to the gardening programme on the other channel.'

'Well, you'll both be disappointed,' says Emma's mother, 'because Emma and I are watching the ballet tonight.'

'It's Swan Lake,' Emma tells her father excitedly. 'When I go to ballet lessons, I'll learn to dance like that.'

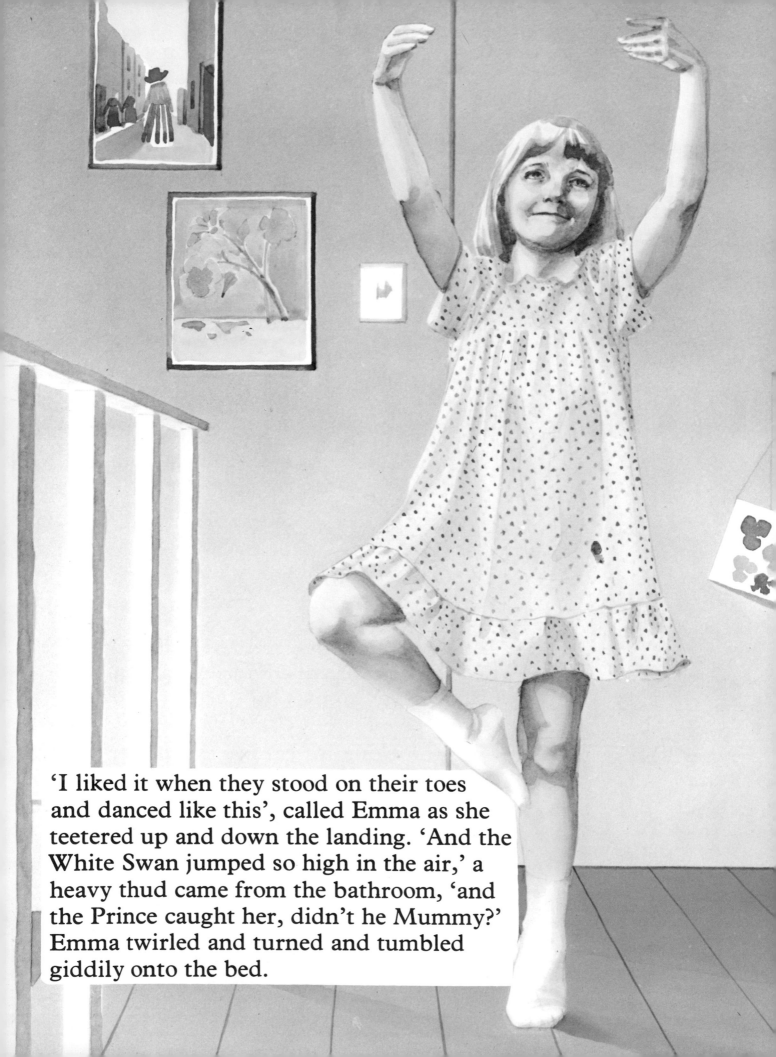

'I liked it when they stood on their toes and danced like this', called Emma as she teetered up and down the landing. 'And the White Swan jumped so high in the air,' a heavy thud came from the bathroom, 'and the Prince caught her, didn't he Mummy?' Emma twirled and turned and tumbled giddily onto the bed.

'In you get,' said her mother firmly. 'Snuggle down and we'll read your book of ballet stories together. Do you remember the tale of "The Firebird?" Here's a picture of the Prince trying to capture the Firebird in the magic garden.'

'Did he rescue the princess?' asked Emma.

'Yes, but first the Firebird helped him to overpower the wicked magician who kept her prisoner.'

Emma and her mother arrived at the studio
in plenty of time.
'We're the audience today,' said Mrs Daley,
'so you'll get a chance to watch all the other
children. Let's sit here out of the way.'

Soon a large group had gathered in the
studio. The children struggled into leotards,
wrestled with the ribbons on their ballet
shoes and swept their hair off their faces with
wide hairbands.

Emma watched the next ten minutes from the side of the piano.

At last she had squirmed her way right onto the floor.

'Join in, Emma,' said Miss Pinkerton, the ballet teacher. 'You can stand behind Jo and copy what she does. At least we won't all trip over you if you're dancing with us.'

The piano played fast music, and all the children shook their wrists and then their ankles. They flopped over and shook from the waists.

'Do you feel all bendy now?' asked Miss Pinkerton.
'Ballet dancers do lots of exercises to loosen their muscles. Let me show you a way of stretching and bending that you can practic at home.'

Soon everybody felt warm and loose, and Miss Pinkerton said it was time to run through some exercises.

She showed them how to place their feet in five different positions. Emma thought Miss Pinkerton looked just like a real dancer making graceful steps.

There were positions for the arms as well. 'Shall we try these?' asked Miss Pinkerton.

Emma practiced first position.

Jo practiced second position.

Mary found third position rather difficult.

And Miss Pinkerton had to show them fourth positions several times.

Everyone managed fifth position. They kept their backs straight and held their arms high.

To finish, Miss Pinkerton asked for some lively music and they all skipped round the hall.

'Come on, Emma,' called her mother, 'did you think the lesson would last all day?'

Emma had hoped it might, but she was looking forward to showing Tom all the steps she had learned.

'Watch me, Tom,' she commanded, 'this is first position.'

'What's that for?' asked Tom.

'It's a position, silly,' said Emma, 'In ballet, all steps begin and end in one of the positions. There are five of them.'

Tom thought she looked pretty silly. He said she ought to be in a circus.

Emma and her mother visited the sportswear department at the local department store. It was full of skates and racquets, football boots and swimming caps.

'A blue leotard for the little girl,' repeated the sales lady and she vanished into a large glass-paned cupboard and looked around in the drawers.

The first leotard was much too baggy, and the
sleeves came down to Emma's knuckles. The
smaller size fitted perfectly and so did the
matching headband.

They spent a long time choosing shoes. Mrs
Daley felt the toes and worried about
Emma's growing feet.
Emma liked the shiny satin ones, but her
mother said, 'Leather shoes or nothing.'

Emma looked at herself in the mirror and
forgot to argue.

Emma wore her new clothes for the second lesson.

She stood at the barre and practised a plié. Slowly she bent her knees, keeping her feet pointed outwards and her back straight.

Miss Pinkerton came to help Jo who was leaning back too far and pushing her stomach forward.

'Arabesque is a beautiful word,' said Miss Pinkerton as she rolled it gently over her tongue. 'Can we all make a shape that's just as lovely, I wonder?'

Emma tried very hard. Slowly she raised her left leg, balancing with outstretched arms.

'I must keep my knees straight,' she thought,
wobbling a little to the right.

'I must keep my head upright,' she thought
wobbling a little to the left.

'Eyes front, Emma,' said Miss Pinkerton,
'Chin up, stomach in.'

The class sat in a circle on the floor, and Miss Pinkerton told them about the concert to be held at the end of term. She told them the story of a magic toyshop where all the toys came to life and danced through the night. The toy soldiers marched in rows to the music of a soldier band. The dolls helped the puppets to move on their strings. Out popped the jack-in-the-box and surprised them all.

Everyone wanted to know what part they would dance.

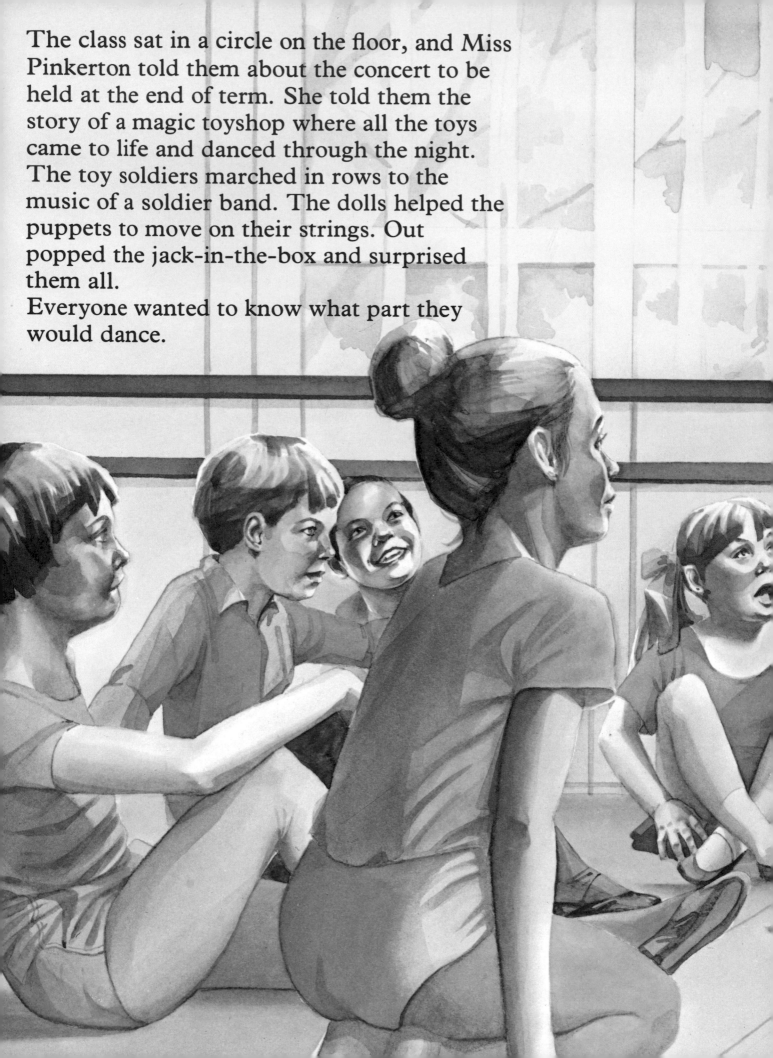

Everybody will join in,' Miss Pinkerton
reassured them, and she promised to tell
them what toy they would act at the next
lesson. 'We will have to work very hard for a
public performance. Each of you
will wear a toy costume and I
hope your parents will
help to make them.'

On Sunday, Emma's family went for a long
walk in the park.
Tom and Emma scrambled over logs and
swung from trees.
They raced through the trees, kicking leaves
to left and right.
At last they collapsed on the ground,
and Emma's mother made a picnic.

'Emma will make a fine dancer with all this exercise and fresh air,' said her father, munching an apple.

'And all this good food,' reminded her mother.

'And what about Tom now,' Emma's father wondered.
'Will he make a fine dancer, too?'

Tom said he would not. He had pinned his hopes on a place in the top football team.

'Well, one thing all athletes need is plenty of sleep,' said Emma's father, 'So it'll be an early night for both of you tonight.'

Mrs Daley planned a special treat for Emma's birthday.

She took Emma and Jo to the theatre to watch the ballet, *Petrouchka*.

The curtain rose on a fairground where a crowd of people were watching a puppet show. The puppeteer pulled the strings to make the toys jerk and act, but soon his magic took over and the puppets came to life.

Petrouchka was a sad clown. He loved the beautiful ballerina who danced at his side, but the puppeteer kept them apart.

Emma dreamed of the lovely ballerina. She looked forward to the concert when she would dance on a stage. She wondered if Miss Pinkerton would choose her as a fairy doll wearing a fluffy tutu covered in sequins that would glitter and sparkle as she moved.

'So Graham and Rosie, you will be tin soldiers, and David will be the jack-in-the-box.' Miss Pinkerton was listing the children's parts. She told several girls that they would be peasant dolls dressed in pinafores and laced dresses.

Emma waited excitedly to hear what part she would dance.

'And Emma,' said Miss Pinkerton, glancing down at her list, 'you will be a rubber ball.'

That night Emma stared hard at herself in the bathroom mirror. How could she dance like a rubber ball? She practised pointing her toes and waving her arms in the air and thought she looked far more like a beautiful fairy doll.

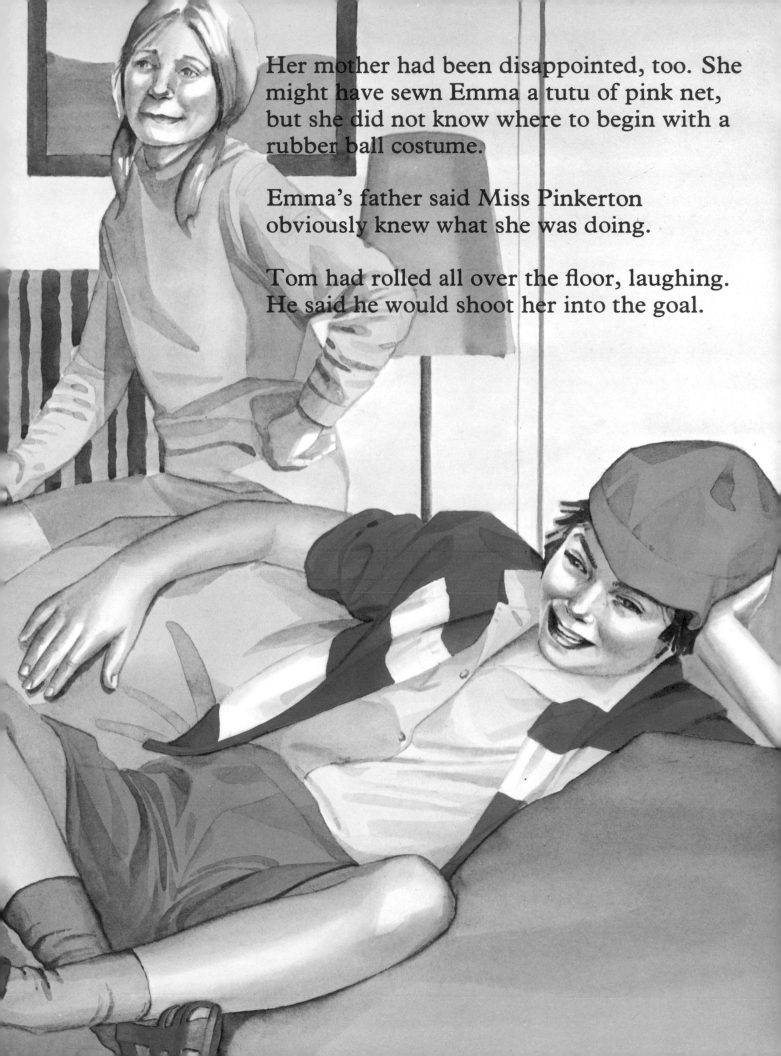

Her mother had been disappointed, too. She might have sewn Emma a tutu of pink net, but she did not know where to begin with a rubber ball costume.

Emma's father said Miss Pinkerton obviously knew what she was doing.

Tom had rolled all over the floor, laughing. He said he would shoot her into the goal.

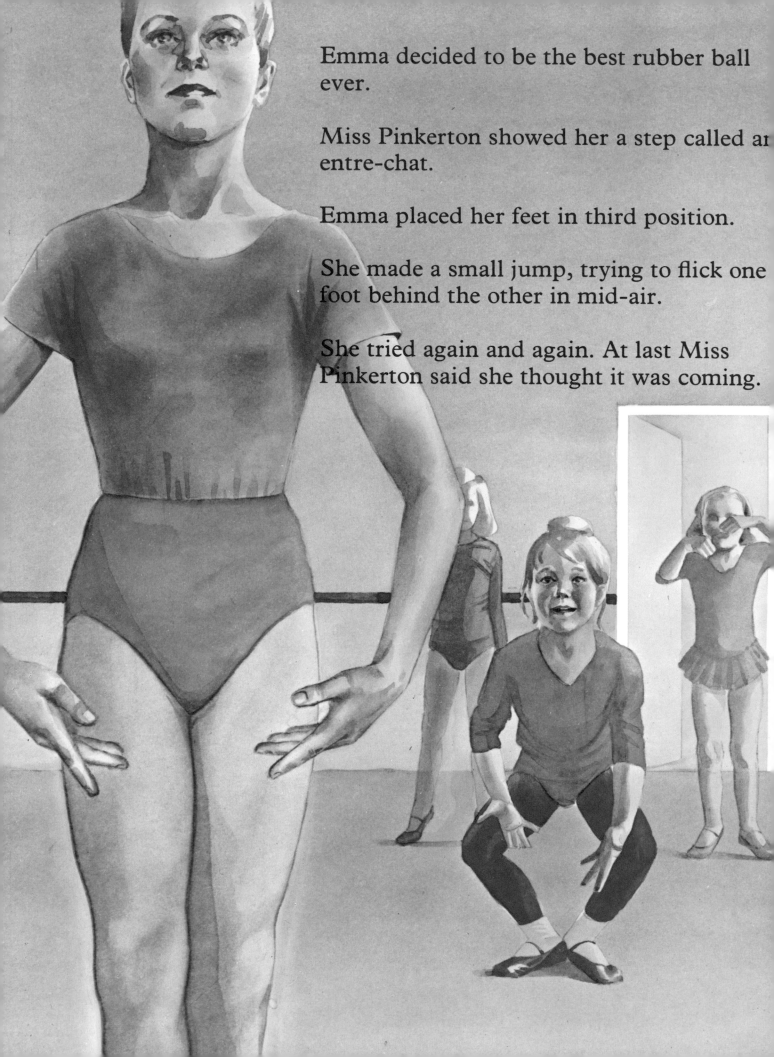

Emma decided to be the best rubber ball ever.

Miss Pinkerton showed her a step called an entre-chat.

Emma placed her feet in third position.

She made a small jump, trying to flick one foot behind the other in mid-air.

She tried again and again. At last Miss Pinkerton said she thought it was coming.

'Try another step,' she suggested. Emma placed her feet in first position and her hands on her hips. She crouched down in a plié, then straightening her knees and pointing her toes, she sprang into the air.

'I hope the audience will clap,'
said Miss Pinkerton. 'I hope they will clap so
loudly that you will all have to take a bow.'

She showed the boys how to stand upright with one hand resting across their stomachs and one behind their backs, and how to bend very slightly from the waist.

The girls learned to curtsey. Stepping to the left and moving their right feet behind the left, they bent slowly at the knee.

Emma learned to curtsey very well. She was hoping to get lots of applause.

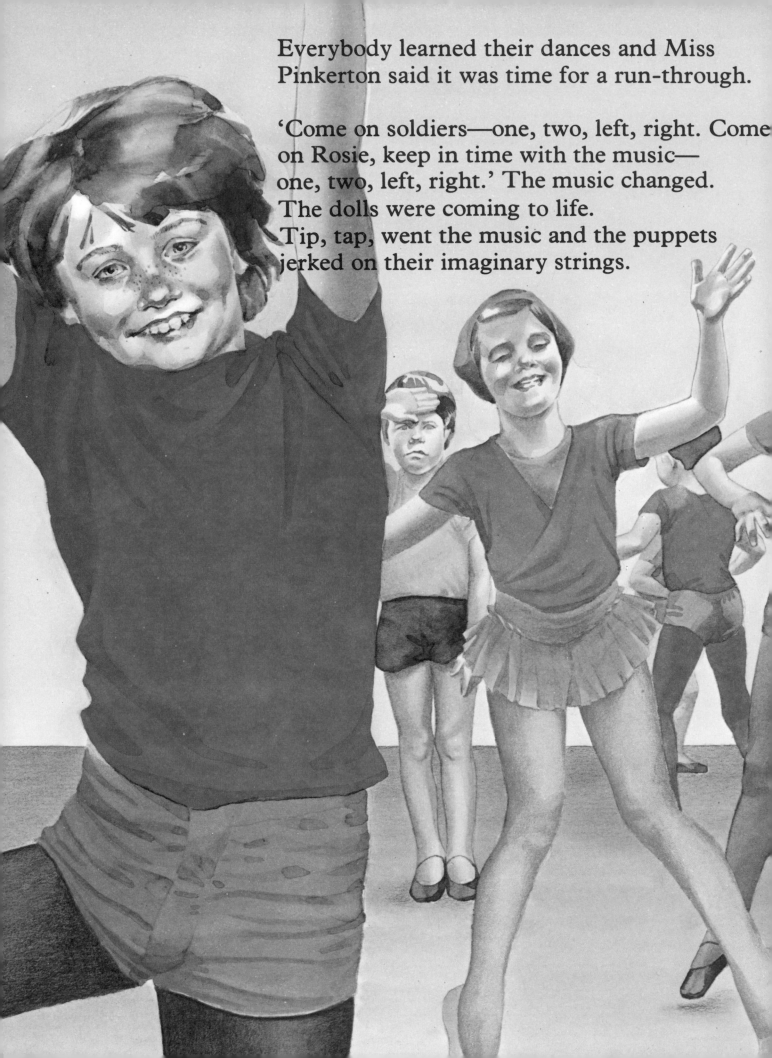

Everybody learned their dances and Miss Pinkerton said it was time for a run-through.

'Come on soldiers—one, two, left, right. Come on Rosie, keep in time with the music— one, two, left, right.' The music changed. The dolls were coming to life.
Tip, tap, went the music and the puppets jerked on their imaginary strings.

Bang! A loud chord on the piano brought the jack-in-the-box leaping from his box. 'Over here, David, now over here,' called Miss Pinkerton.

The toys danced together in a waltz. Emma thought they looked wonderful. She liked the music, too.

As the sounds died away, all the toys went back to sleep.

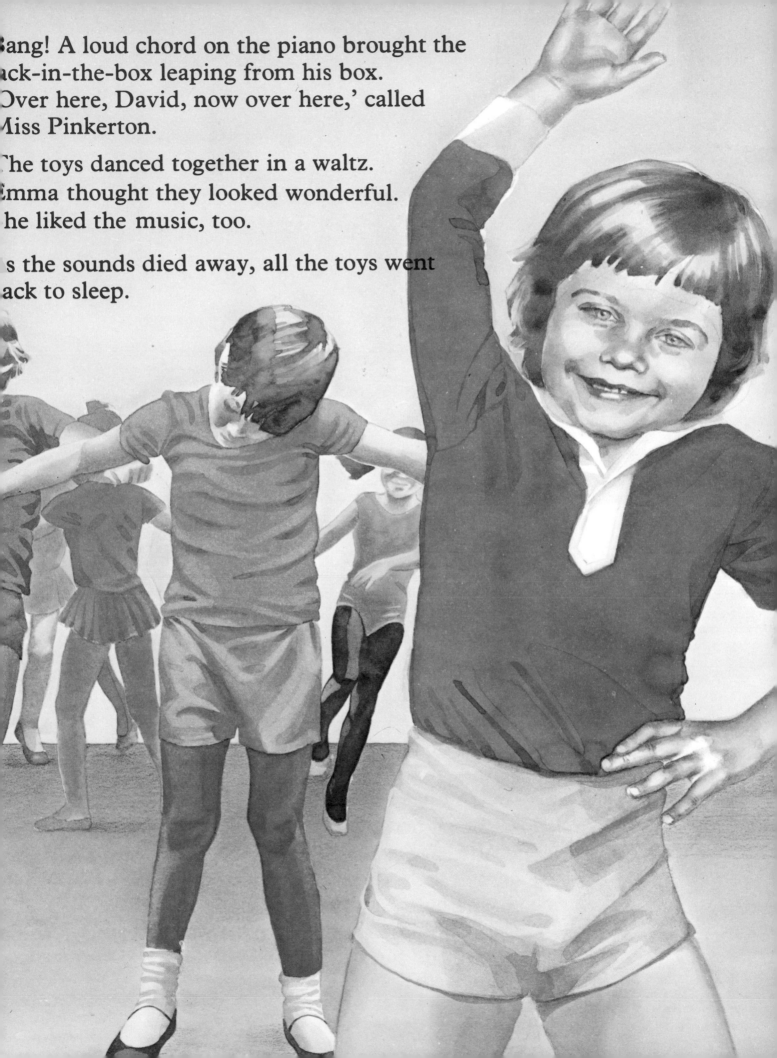

Mrs Daley helped Jo's mother to sew a fairy doll costume.

'If only Emma could have been a fairy doll,' she sighed. 'I'm having such problems with all that foam rubber.'

She cut a strip of pink net and stitched it carefully in gathers. Jo's mother seamed the satin bodice.

Does Jo carry a wand?' asked Mrs Daley.

o's father had made the wand. He had made
sequined headdress from a piece of wire.
Now he was down at the centre painting the
cenery.

Emma's father promised to go down and
end a hand the moment his television
programme was finished.

When all the costumes were finished, Miss Pinkerton held a dress rehearsal. The children practised on the big stage at the centre. It had full blue curtains and real spotlights overhead.

Everyone was excited. Miss Pinkerton said she had never seen them dance so badly.

'Oh dear,' she whispered to the piano lady, 'Will they ever get it right?'

Emma's
mother was excited, too.
She and Emma looked through
the ballet book until they found
pictures of '*La Boutique Fantasque.*'

'This is a ballet about a magic toyshop just like yours,' she said. Imagine my little daughter dancing on the stage. Miss Pinkerton says you've worked very hard at your lessons. We're all looking forward to the concert.'

The children stood in the wings behind the curtain and listened to the chatter from the audience. They watched the electrician on his ladder as he adjusted the lights. They watched the piano lady sorting through her music and Miss Pinkerton talking to a photographer.

He promised to take a photo of the magic toyshop dance.

Miss Pinkerton told them to jump up and down on the spot.

'Keep loose and make those muscles warm up.'

Emma was so scared she could not loosen up at all.

'Off we go,' said Miss Pinkerton, and the piano lady played the first chord. The children ran on stage and took up their positions.